beecuus

To

D.T

HUNKLUBEbB

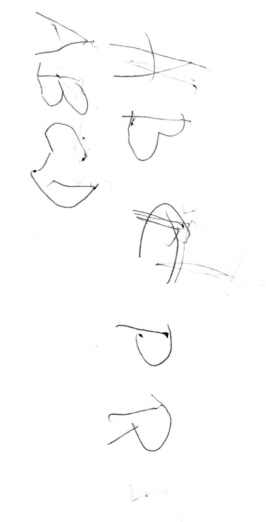

Yes, I Can!

Dedicated to
my favorite twin brother,
Dr. David Phillips,
from Doris.

Yes, I Can!

CHALLENGING CEREBRAL PALSY

BY DORIS SANFORD
ILLUSTRATIONS BY GRACI EVANS

MULTNOMAH PRESS

Stacy sat in the corner of the giant lobby. She could hear it now: "What did you do in Hawaii, Stacy?"

"Sat in the hotel lobby."

She didn't blame Lindy for leaving. Scuba diving and playing on the beach would definitely be more fun than pushing someone around in a wheelchair. But Lindy was her guest, and more important, she was her friend. Lindy wouldn't be here if Stacy's parents hadn't said it was okay to bring a friend. Her parents had won an all-expense-paid trip to this fancy hotel in Hawaii. Lindy was having the time of her life and Stacy was sitting in the corner of the lobby.

She turned to leave, and there he was! Not only the cutest guy she had ever seen, but an honest-to-goodness movie star. His pictures were all over her bedroom wall. She couldn't believe it when he smiled and walked over.

An hour later she had made a friend. She told him about being left behind and he asked if having a ticket to his concert that night would help. "Yes, it *would* help!" She could hardly wait.

He leaned over and looked Stacy in the eye, "You know Stacy, sometimes people like me for the wrong reasons, and sometimes people reject you for the wrong reasons, but don't let those people be in charge of your attitude. See you tonight." And he was gone.

The concert was wonderful. Stacy had a front-row seat! But the letters, autographed pictures, and phone calls after she got home were the *best!*

Going home meant going back to Holladay Center School for children with disabilities. Stacy had been there since she was three years old. She wasn't "different" at Holladay Center. Many of the other children also had cerebral palsy. School wasn't easy and learning to read was especially hard, but she liked being with her friends.

She remembered one discussion in her classroom. The teacher had asked what each of the children wanted to do when they grew up. Stacy said she wanted to be a model. Everyone laughed and someone said, "Be *real*, Stace." She *was* being real.

Then the teacher said, "Stacy, is there anything else you would like to do when you grow up?"

Stacy answered, "Be a model who is a mother." The teacher said that would be nice and Stacy knew she meant that it would be nice if it were possible, but it wasn't possible. Stacy thought, "Oh, yes I can. Just wait and see!"

One of the boys said he wanted to be an astronaut because in space there weren't any barriers. The teacher said, "There don't have to be any on earth, either." Stacy wished *she* had said something wise like that!

9

One day at Holladay Center, a camera crew arrived and several of the children were told they could be stars in a film to demonstrate how P.E. teachers could help children with disabilities. Stacy could be one of those stars if she wanted. She said yes *before* she learned that all of the children in the film would receive fifty dollars. She knew movie stars were rich, and now she was rich!

At home that night she overheard a conversation between her parents about a family at their church who needed money. When she received her fifty dollars, Stacy put the money in an envelope marked, "For that family. Don't tell it's from me." She knew her parents would let her help the family. Her parents were like that. They adopted Stacy's older brother Kevin, and three years later, adopted her. Brian, who was a foster child, was almost like a brother because he had lived with them since he was eight years old.

Stacy remembered once overhearing someone say to her parents, "You're such saints." Her parents were too polite to laugh, but when they got in the car, her dad said, "Sure we're saints, and you three are angels." They all laughed.

Stacy knew that sometimes it was hard for her brothers to deal with her disability. Helping Stacy took extra time. Sometimes the boys weren't quite sure what their parents expected, and sometimes they felt guilty about going outside to play with their friends when Stacy couldn't play with them. She was glad that her parents told her brothers to go and play, and thanked her brothers often when they helped. Stacy was glad, too, that her parents told the boys that nothing they had done had caused the cerebral palsy.

Stacy's parents had learned about the cerebral palsy when she was nine months old. They hadn't been surprised. They had known something wasn't right. They also knew that finding the cause of her problems was not going to make the problems go away.

By the time she was twelve years old, Stacy had two addresses—one at home and the other her "home away from home," the children's hospital. So far she'd had six operations. Some of the operations were serious and some were not-so-serious. She wasn't afraid of going to the hospital except when she had to have a cast removed. Everyone promised that it wouldn't hurt, but you never know!

Saturdays were the hardest days at the hospital. Most kids got to go home on pass for the day. After previous surgeries she had gone home too, but not this time.

She wondered why some of her friends said they were afraid to come to the hospital and see her. Nothing bad would happen to *them!* And besides, she couldn't visit them—she had a new body cast! This operation was performed to fix her hip bones.

Jesse, her Golden Retriever, had his hips operated on the same week. People teased, "Does he have to do *everything* with you?" She wondered how he would be able to jump up on her bed when she got home. She was used to his warm fur on her toes at night. At least she understood why she was having this operation. Jesse didn't know what was happening to him. Poor Jesse.

One day a man from United Cerebral Palsy came to talk to her at the hospital. He said he was there to ask a favor. Stacy replied, "Sure, anything I can do flat on my back!"

"No, Stacy, after you are out of the hospital and back in your wheelchair, would you be the co-host for the United Cerebral Palsy telethon on TV?"

She didn't have to think about *that* for very long! The next day in the hospital, Stacy thought about what she would say on television. She would say that some people have a crippling disability called *prejudice*. She would tell them that she was more like other children than different from them. She had belonged to Blue Birds, was Snow White in the school play, would be taking horseback riding lessons soon, and was a volunteer at the local hospital. She would tell them about taking dance classes in her power chair and how good it felt when her dance teacher yelled at her like he yelled at the other kids. She would tell them that taking piano lessons was hard work for everyone, disabled or not.

She would tell them that she was happy her parents could park in the handicapped parking slots at the shopping mall because it meant that she could start spending money before other kids! She would tell them that having cerebral palsy was not a big deal; it was just who she was, but that it did hurt her feelings when people asked her mother, "What does she want?" instead of asking Stacy. She would say that sometimes people called her special, but she didn't want to be special. Being Stacy was special enough and *that* would be enough to say!

All that thinking made her tired and soon she was asleep. She woke up to a terrible tickle. With one eye open she could see Lisa, her best friend, standing at the foot of her bed, feather in hand. Lisa was the kind of friend who could wake you up with a feather or sit quietly and listen for hours. That's what best friends do and Lisa was a *great* best friend.

Lisa was a person who could ignore the wheelchair and see her friend. She didn't answer questions that didn't have answers, such as, "Why did God make me this way?" "What will happen to me if my parents die?" "Why doesn't God make me better when I pray so hard that He will?"

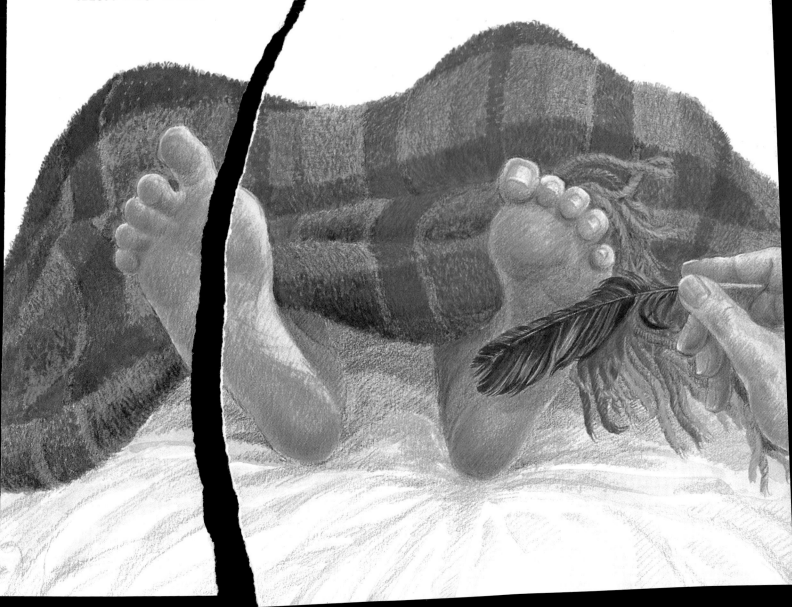

Lisa would just tell Stacy, "You don't know what's ahead. Maybe there will be some surprises you don't expect." That seemed like a good answer.

Most of the time, the two of them just talked and played and laughed. For instance, one day they went shopping at the sidewalk sale and one of the clothes racks caught the back of Stacy's wheelchair. As she moved away she pulled the rack of clothes behind her. Everyone was laughing, especially Stacy.

Another time when it was raining hard Lisa's parents drove the girls to the mall. Stacy's car door was not shut and Lisa's parents asked her to run around and shut the door. Lisa said she didn't want to get wet. Stacy's disability was no reason to wreck a perfectly good hairstyle!

Jim and Steve were special friends, too. They were grown-up and played soccer on a professional team. Because Stacy had developed a friendship with the owner of the team while she was exercising at the athletic club, she had been invited to sit near the bench during games.

After games, Jim and Steve teased her and talked awhile. Jim even took her for a long ride in his sports car with her wheelchair hanging out the back. When Stacy went to the hospital, Jim and Steve came to visit. No matter what kind of a day it had been, it suddenly got better when Steve and Jim came around. The fact that they were handsome and all the other girls were jealous didn't hurt a bit!

Stacy had participated in Special Olympics for as long as she could remember. She liked to save the purple, red, and blue ribbons and hang them on her wall at home. She remembered one of the coaches telling her not to let others decide her limits because if *you* don't take a chance on your dreams, who will? Not bad advice, whether or not you got a blue ribbon.

Stacy loved competition. Tummy-scooter races, softball, bean-bag throws—all the games were fun. No one was a loser at Special Olympics, and all of the victories were celebrated.

The first day at public school was a day to remember! She was sure it was going to be difficult when the wheel came off of her power chair that morning and she had to go to school in her manual chair. Asking strangers to push you on the first day of junior high is not cool! It was bad enough that she had to be in eighth grade for two years. She had to skip seventh grade because the classroom was upstairs and she couldn't get there! Oh well, she would make the best of it.

But five minutes into her first class, the kid next to her said, "What's the matter with you, anyway?" And before she could answer, the girl in front of him said, "She's crippled, can't you see?" The rest of the day was just surviving until it was time to go home.

When Stacy was safe on her bed that afternoon, she cried. Jesse licked her tears as fast as they fell. When she was finally tired of dog breath, she decided she had better stop crying and figure out what to do.

What *could* she do?

She could *teach* them, that's what! The following morning she asked her homeroom teacher if she could explain to the class about her cerebral palsy. The teacher said yes.

So, the teacher told the class, "Stacy has something to share with you." For once Stacy was glad that she was sitting down. It was harder for them to see her knees knocking that way. She began, "I'm Stacy and I have cerebral palsy. It's not contagious; it just affects my ability to move *and* it affects my being accepted by other people who don't understand. Cerebral palsy has also affected my speech, so you have to work a little harder to understand what I have to say, but in most ways I am like you.

"If you want to help me, you can let me study from your class notes because I have difficulty writing. You

can also help me by pushing me wheelchair when my power chair is broken, like it was yesterday.

"I make a very good friend and it's okay to ask me questions about my disability. You can't learn about it unless you ask. It's not wrong to be curious about something that you don't understand." Then she flashed her big Stacy smile and wheeled over to her spot at the side of the room. The teacher said, "Thanks, Stacy," and it was over.

After class two girls came over and said, "Hi! Can we walk with you to your next class?" It looked like the beginning.

Stacy missed her friends at Holladay Center. After graduation all of her friends had gone to various public schools. She imagined what it was like for them— probably no easier than it was for her. Her disability sometimes separated her from her new friends because she couldn't always go where they went. It was such a hassle to go someplace.

But one place she did go was dances. Nobody went to more dances than Stacy. All of the boys from Holladay Center knew she liked to dance, so she was invited to every prom at their schools.

Once when she was sitting on the sidelines near a friend, she said, "I wonder if these boys ask me to dance because they feel sorry about my disability." And her friend said, "Oh, Stacy, they ask you to dance because you are so pretty, and because you're a great dancer, and because you're fun to be around. I wish I had the close friendships that you have!"

It was early morning and Stacy was sleepy. She tried to hurry with her usual routine. This was no ordinary day and she did not want to be late. Her dad would drive her. Junior Fashion Modeling School had accepted her. She could model scarves, hats, and blouses. Yes, I can! Yes, I can! she sang to herself.

She remembered that afternoon when she had told the class that she wanted to be a model and they had said, "Get real." Well, she *was* getting real, all the way to the modeling school! This was the first step in reaching her dream.

"Look out world; here I come!"

Discussion Questions

1. What is the name of Stacy's disability?

2. Name one thing Stacy couldn't do because of her disability and two things she could do.

3. What do you wish everyone knew about people with disabilities?

4. Stacy said she didn't want to be called special. Why not?

5. If you want to know more about a certain disability, how could you find out?

6. How could you have helped Stacy if you had gone to the same school?

7. How could Stacy have helped *you*?

A B C D E F G H I J K L M N O P Q R S T U V W X

A B C D E F G H I J K L M N O P Q R S T U V W X